THE
PHOTO
NOVEL

MVFOL

TWENTIETH CENTURY FOX PRESENTS IN ASSOCIATION WITH CONSTANTIN FILM AND MARVEL ENTERPRISES, INC.
A 1492 PICTURES / BERND EICHINGER PRODUCTION "FANTASTIC FOUR" IOAN GRUFFUDD JESSICA ALBA CHRIS EVANS MICHAEL CHIKLIS
JULIAN McMAHON KERRY WASHINGTON MUSIC BY JOHN OTTMAN MUSIC SUPERVISOR DAVE JORDAN CO-PRODUCER ROSS FANGER FILM EDITOR WILLIAM HOY A.C.E.
PRODUCTION DESIGNER BILL BOES DIRECTION OF PHOTOGRAPHY OLIVER WOOD EXECUTIVE PRODUCERS STAN LEE KEVIN FEIGE CHRIS COLUMBUS MARK RADCLIFFE MICHAEL BARNATHAN
PRODUCED BY BERND EICHINGER AVI ARAD RALPH WINTER BASED ON THE MARVEL COMIC BOOK BY STAN LEE AND JACK KIRBY WRITTEN BY MARK FROST AND MICHAEL FRANCE DIRECTED BY TIM STORY

MARVEL   PG-13 PARENTS STRONGLY CAUTIONED
Some Material May Be Inappropriate for Children Under 13
Sequences of Intense Action and Some Suggestive Content

ORIGINAL SOUNDTRACK AVAILABLE ON WIND-UP RECORDS   SCORE ALBUM AVAILABLE ON
www.fantasticfourmovie.com

HarperCollins®, ☎®, and HarperKidsEntertainment™
are trademarks of HarperCollins Publishers.

FANTASTIC FOUR: THE PHOTO NOVEL

For information address HarperCollins Children's Books, a division of
HarperCollins Publishers, 1350 Avenue of the Americas, New York, NY 10019.
Library of Congress catalog card number: 2005930852
ISBN-10: 0-06-085378-6—ISBN-13: 978-0-06-085378-5
www.harperchildrens.com
www.fantasticfourmovie.com
www.marvel.com
Book design by Joe Merkel

❖

FANTASTIC 4

THE PHOTO NOVEL

ADAPTED BY **DAVID SEIDMAN**
BASED ON THE MOTION PICTURE WRITTEN BY
MARK FROST AND **MICHAEL FRANCE**

HarperKidsEntertainment
An Imprint of HarperCollins*Publishers*

...ALL THE WAY TO THE *LAUNCH SITE*.

VONDOOM
AEROSPACE

THE KID WAS A *PAIN*.

THE LOOK ON YOUR FACE WHEN YOU FOUND OUT YOU'RE MY *JUNIOR* OFFICER... PRICELESS.

HIS BIG *SISTER*, THOUGH...

4

6

...MY FIANCÉE, *DEBBIE.*

I'LL BE WATCHING OVER YOU FROM SPACE.

JUST GET BACK SOON.

WHILE I FOCUSED ON DEB, *REED* WAS MORE INTERESTED IN *SUE*...

...WHO WAS GLUED TO VICTOR'S EVERY *WORD.*

THE MAP OF THE PAST WILL CHART THE PATH OF THE *FUTURE!*

NOW, IF YOU'LL EXCUSE ME—

HISTORY AWAITS!

SO UP WE GO ON THE *SHUTTLE* TO VICTOR'S *SPACE STATION.*

I'M SUPPOSED TO PUT SOME *PLANTS* OUT IN SPACE. REED WANTED TO SEE WHAT THE STORM'S *COSMIC RAYS* WOULD DO TO STUFF THAT'S *ALIVE.*

10

YOU'RE *DONE*, TRUST ME. THE *STORM'S* COMING!

ROGER THAT. ON MY WAY.

JOHNNY... REED... *HURRY*.

IT'S TOO LATE FOR THEM.

WHAT ARE YOU *DOING*?

I'M RAISING THE SHIELDS AROUND THIS ROOM. YOU AND I WILL BE *SAFE*.

THAT'S WHEN SUE RAN TO *REED* AND *JOHNNY*!

YOU CAN'T LEAVE THEM *OUT* THERE!

DON'T BE *STUPID*, SUE.

YOU CAN'T *HELP* THEM!

BUT ALL OF A SUDDEN...

THE RAYS SHOT THROUGH THE *SHUTTLE* AND BLEW UP A *CONTROL PANEL* NEAR *VIC!*

THEY HIT *REED* WHILE HE WAS REACHING TO LET ME BACK IN!

THEY TORE INTO **SUE**—AND INTO A METAL PIPE THAT SPAT **INVISIBLE GASES** AT HER!

THEY BURNED **JOHNNY**—AND MADE A MACHINE NEAR HIM **BURST INTO FLAME!**

AND *ME*... I FELT *JOHNNY* AND *REED* PULLING ME *INSIDE*...

HE'S NOT RESPONDING—

...WHILE...

BEN! *BEN!*

.../...

...PASSED...

...OUT!

NEXT THING I KNEW—

—I HEARD *JOHNNY* AGAIN.

BEN, WAKE *UP!*
WE'RE BACK ON EARTH—
VICTOR'S *MEDICAL*
CENTER.

WHERE'S *REED?*
AND *SUE?*

SUE... I'M *SORRY*.

I'M NOT SURE WHICH ONE OF THEM FELT *WORSE*.

JOHNNY, THOUGH— HE WAS DOING *GREAT*.

DOCTOR'S ORDERS— YOU'RE NOT ALLOWED TO *LEAVE*. YOU FEEL *FEVERISH*.

I'VE NEVER FELT *BETTER*.

THE SLICKEST SKI RUN THIS SIDE OF THE *ALPS* IS RIGHT *OUTSIDE*. MEET ME AT THE *TOP*!

WHILE JOHNNY WAS RUNNING *HOT* AND *COLD*...

THAT NIGHT, SUE WAS FEELING BETTER, SO I GOT HER TO MEET ME AT VON DOOM'S *DINING HALL*.

I CAN'T STAY *LONG*, BEN. I PROMISED *VICTOR* I'D MEET HIM FOR *DINNER*.

ABSOLUTELY— HEY, ISN'T THAT *REED*?

HEY, *REED*—

20

WHY DON'T YOU *JOIN* US?

REED DIDN'T **KNOW** I SET THE WHOLE THING UP—BUT HE LOOKED PRETTY HAPPY TO SEE **SUE**.

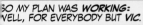

SO MY PLAN WAS **WORKING:** WELL, FOR EVERYBODY BUT **VIC**.

E WAS WAITING FOR SUE...

...BUT WHILE HE WAS **WAITING**, HE FOCUSED ON **HIMSELF**.

I'VE **GOT TO** DO SOMETHING ABOUT THIS **SCAR**.

THAT'S WHEN VIC'S EMPLOYEE, **LEONARD**, PIPED UP.

IT'S NICE TO BE WANTED... TO BE HEARD... SEEN...
SUE...
LOOK DOWN.
SHE COULDN'T BELIEVE SHE WAS DISAPPEARING.
SHE JUMPED UP AND KNOCKED A BOTTLE OFF THE TABLE...

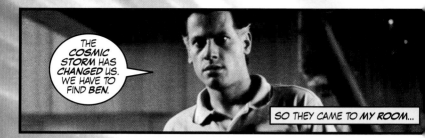

THE *COSMIC STORM* HAS *CHANGED* US. WE HAVE TO FIND *BEN.*

SO THEY CAME TO *MY ROOM...*

BUT I JUST TOLD THEM TO LEAVE ME *ALONE!*

NEXT THING I KNEW, REED'S *HAND* WAS SQUEEZING UNDER MY *DOOR...*

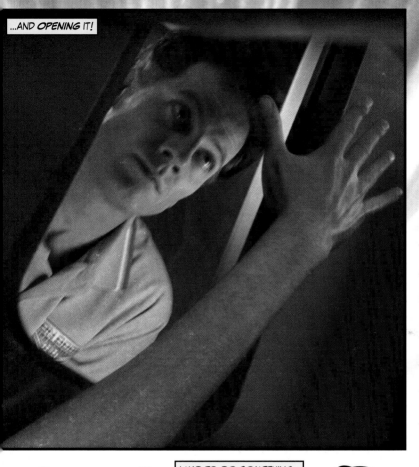

...AND *OPENING* IT!

I HAD TO *DO* SOMETHING...

I WENT TO THE **ONE PERSON** WHO I **KNEW** WANTED TO SEE ME.

I WASN'T SURE **HOW** TO LET HER SEE ME, THOUGH, SO I HID IN THE SHADOWS AND CALLED UP TO HER.

DEB... IT'S **ME**.

BEN? YOU HOME, BABY?

THIS IS GONNA BE KIND OF A **SHOCK**...

REMEMBER WHEN WE SAID WE'D BE **TOGETHER** NO MATTER **WHAT**?

IT SURE WAS.

DON'T...

DON'T...

DON'T **TOUCH** ME!

BUT, I...

PERFECT. THANKS.

I GUESS THE WAY I LOOKED *SCARED* A GUY, 'CAUSE ALL OF A *SUDDEN*...

...HE FELL OFF THE *BRIDGE!*

I HAD TO *SAVE* THE GUY!

THE LOUSY TRUCK WAS GOING TOO *FAST!* EVEN AFTER IT *HIT* ME, IT KEPT *GOING*...

...AND CAUSED A PILEUP.

T ONE OF HER FORCE FIELDS NCHED INTO A FIRE TRUCK...
FIRE
...AND KNOCKED IT OFF THE BRIDGE!
THE FIREMEN WERE GONNA FALL INTO THE RIVER...
...SO I HAD TO LEND A HAND!
IT WASN'T EASY.
URGH!

MEANWHILE, REED WAS TAKING *FOREVER* TO *FIX* ME. I WAS GETTING *ANTSY* COOPED UP IN HIS LAB. I HAD TO GO SOMEPLACE THAT FELT LIKE *HOME*.

LIKE MY OLD HAUNT, *O'DONNELL'S PUB.*

JUST THE *SIGHT* OF ME MADE EVERYBODY CLEAR OUT...

...EVERYBODY BUT *ONE*.

WHY ARE *YOU* STILL HERE? DIDN'T MY LOOKS SOBER YOU UP?

THEN I *GOT* IT...

I HOPE YOU TWO ARE *HAPPY* TOGETHER.

YOU'RE FINALLY *PERFECT* FOR HIM... BECAUSE YOU'RE *INVISIBLE*.

JOHNNY WASN'T INVISIBLE, THOUGH. OR *QUIET*, EITHER.

REED TOLD US TO STAY IN HIS *LAB* COMPLEX UNTIL HE COULD BUILD A MACHINE TO *FIX* US—

—BUT *JOHNNY* JUST HAD TO *SHOW OFF*.

AND NOW— LADIES AND GENTLEMEN, THE *ESPN MOTO X GAMES* HAS A *SPECIAL TREAT* FOR YOU...

VRRROOOM!

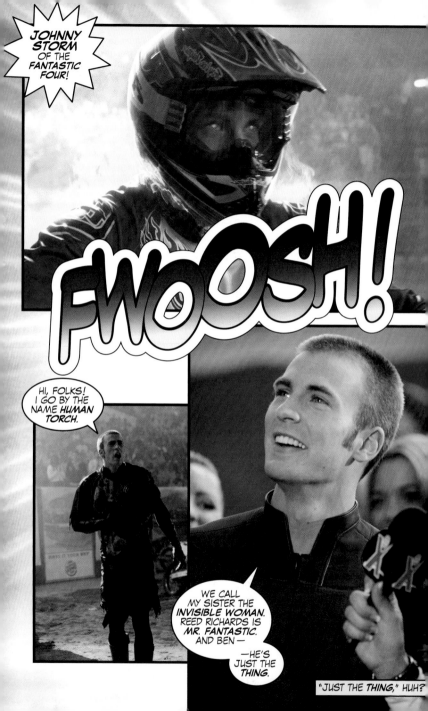

AFTER *THAT*, I JUST *LEFT*.

BUT ON TV, *VIC* SAW WHAT WE DID, AND SO DID HIS *BANKER*. VIC FOUND THE GUY IN THE BANK'S *PARKING GARAGE*...

VON *DOOM*?

...WHERE NOBODY COULD *SEE* THEM.

YOU GAVE ME A LITTLE *SHOCK*.

REED RICHARDS AND HIS *FREAKS* ARE KILLING YOUR COMPANY. MY BANK'S PULLING *OUT* OF VON DOOM INDUSTRIES.

S C R A C K L E

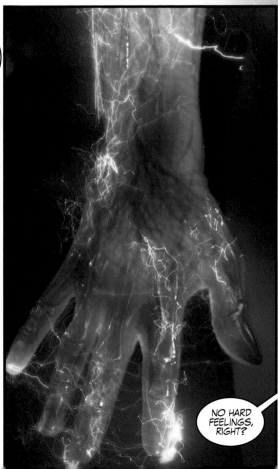

NO HARD FEELINGS, RIGHT?

SO THE NEXT MORNING, WHEN REED WAS UP IN HIS *LAB*, WORKING ON A MACHINE TO CHANGE US ALL *BACK*...

VICTOR?

WHAT ARE YOU *DOING* HERE?

WHAT I *SHOULD* HAVE DONE A LONG TIME AGO.

THIS *MACHINE* YOU'RE BUILDING TO RE-CREATE THE *COSMIC STORM* AND REVERSE ITS *EFFECTS*—

MY MEN CAN *MASS-PRODUCE* IT.

BUT I NEED TIME TO...

I'M NOT ASKING *PERMISSION*.

AND THAT WAS IT. VIC *LEFT*.

REED JUST WENT BACK TO *WORK*.

THEN *SUE* CAME IN.

...AND THEY *TALKED*... AND *TALKED*...

...AND THEN THEY *STOPPED* TALKING.

NOW, *ME*—I JUST WANTED TO BE *ALONE*. SO I TOOK A *WALK*.

HELP!

IT WAS A LITTLE *KID*...AND HER *CAT* WAS UP A *TREE*.

MEEOOWWRR...

SO I GAVE THE TREE A *SHAKE*—

AND DOWN CAME THE *CAT*... AND THAT WAS *THAT*.

THANK YOU, THANK YOU, THANK YOU!

I DIDN'T KNOW WHAT TO *SAY*.

THE KID COULD *SEE* ME...

...BUT SHE DIDN'T TREAT ME LIKE A *MONSTER*.

...OTHER THAN GETTING CLOSER TO *SUE*?

REED SAID IT'D BE *WEEKS* 'TIL—

I SAY HIS MACHINE IS READY *NOW*.

DO YOU WANT TO BE *BEN GRIMM* AGAIN?

LET'S *DO* IT.

SO WE WENT TO REED'S *LAB*...

...AND HIS *TRANSFORMATION MACHINE.*

I GOT IN, AND VIC TURNED IT *ON.*

I COULD HEAR THE *POWER* RISE...

E WAS GONNA HURT **REED**, **JOHNNY**, AND **SUE**. AND IT WAS ALL **MY FAULT!**

I HAD TO **STOP** HIM!

BUT I FELT SO **DRAINED**, SO **WEAK**.

BEN?

AND THEN **SUE**...

...AND **JOHNNY** SHOWED UP. I GUESS MY CHANGE BACK TO **NORMAL** MADE A **COMMOTION**, SO THEY CAME TO SEE WHAT WAS GOING ON.

WHERE IS REED?

VICTOR MUST'VE GOTTEN HIM.

VIC HAD GOTTEN **REED**, ALL RIGHT... BUT HE'D ALSO GOTTEN A **MASK!**
I GUESS HE DIDN'T LIKE HIS SCARRED-UP **FACE**.
AND NOW VIC WAS CALLING HIMSELF **DOCTOR DOOM**.
BASIC CHEMISTRY, REED...

MORE *EXACTLY...* JOHNNY!

GREAT. A *HEAT*-SEEKING MISSILE.

HE HAD NO PLACE TO GO BUT *DOWN.*

AND HE FELL...
AND BURST INTO FLAME...
RRRROAR
AND FLEW! THE KID COULD FLY!

THE MISSILE **LOCKED ON** TO HIM...

M   48.50.40
E   28.23.20
ALT   308
KGS   1636
DIVE +   4

25
20
15
10
5
0
-5
-10
-15
-20
-25

+70

VVROOSH

...AND YOU SHOULD'VE
SEEN THE KID **GO**!

HE ZIGGED—

ROOOSSSHHH!

AND *ZAGGED*—

FFROOM!

—AND SHE WHIPPED UP A *FORCE FIELD* TO HIT HIM!

...YOU ALWAYS THOUGHT YOU WERE *GOD.*

BUT VIC JUST SET HIMSELF UP TO DO SOMETHING *NASTY.*

SUSAN...

...YOU'RE *FIRED.*

SCRRRRRAKAKAKA

IT'S CLOBBERIN' TIME!

YEAH, I WENT BACK TO REED'S *LAB* AND TURNED BACK INTO *THE THING!*

I DIDN'T *WANT TO.* I WOULD'VE GIVEN *ANYTHING* TO STAY *BEN* AND NEVER BE THE *THING* AGAIN. BUT I GAVE VIC THE POWER TO DESTROY MY *FRIENDS—* AND I HAD TO *SAVE* THEM!

AND SO...

BAM!

I HIT VIC SO HARD, HE FLEW INTO THE *WALL!*

HE STOPPED MOVING, AND I TURNED TO *REED.*

PUM!

BOY, I'VE BEEN WAITING TO DO THAT.

BUT I HEARD SOMETHING *BEHIND* ME.

IT WAS *VIC.* HE WOULDN'T STAY *DOWN!*

CRZACK!

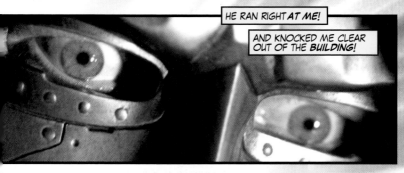

HE RAN RIGHT *AT ME!*

AND KNOCKED ME CLEAR OUT OF THE *BUILDING!*

WE HIT THE *STREET* OUTSIDE. IT WASN'T EASY FOR ME TO GET *UP* AFTER THAT...

...BUT *VIC* DIDN'T HAVE ANY PROBLEM.

I DIDN'T KNOW WHAT HE WAS *DOING*...

78

AND WHEN I HIT THE *GROUND*—

—LOOK WHAT I SAW LOOKING *DOWN* AT ME!

VIC—

THIS IS WHO WE ARE. *WE* CAN ACCEPT IT.

AND MAYBE EVEN—

—ALL THE WAY ON!

I DIDN'T KNOW THE KID HAD THAT MUCH *IN* HIM!

BUT *REED* KNEW— AND HE WASN'T *DONE!*

SUE —
YOU KNOW
WHAT TO
DO.

SUE RAISED A *FORCE FIELD*
AROUND JOHNNY'S FLAME —
AND TRAPPED *VIC* IN IT!

BUT WHEN IT WAS
ALL *OVER*...

—AND *FROZE VIC SOLID!*